T0368427

MY JEANS?

Dr. Dawn Diehnelt

Illustrated by Toffee Maja Gluchowska

Balboa Press books may be ordered through booksellers or by contacting:

Balboa Press
A Division of Hay House
1663 Liberty Drive
Bloomington, IN 47403
www.balboapress.com
844-682-1282

ISBN: 979-8-7652-4935-2 (sc)
ISBN: 979-8-7652-4936-9 (e)

Library of Congress Control Number: 2024901973

Print information available on the last page.

Balboa Press rev. date: 03/18/2024

BALBOA.PRESS
A DIVISION OF HAY HOUSE

"I love this book. The graphics are excellent. The boy's lips are open on nearly every page. Let's get it into every parents hands and make it the #1 best seller."

— **Cheri Meyer** RDH, OMT

My Jeans? explains a common childhood concern that many children have in a relatable, cute story with great, modern pictures. Dr. Dawn Diehnelt, DDS educates and entertains with this story for children of all ages."

— **Author Margaret Kay,** mother and grandmother

"In this book, Dr. Diehnelt answered one of the most common questions in orthodontics: What is the cause of crooked teeth? She presents the answer in a very entertaining way. And not only that. Dr. Diehnelt shows how concepts can be misunderstood and lead the public into a total wrong way. But at the end the reader will understand the cause of crooked teeth, the cells in our body react and respond to whatever is happening in their neighborhood. And, it is explained in a very simple and funny way."

— **German Ramirez-Yanez DDS, MDsc, MSc, PhD**

"Great book. The kids really loved it."

— **Carol Galat,** mother and grandmother

"Anytime we can help eliminate confusion, we should take it. This is especially true when teaching scientific concepts to elementary to middle school children. Dr. Diehnelt has written an easy-to-follow story that explains why teeth get crooked. The relationship with family members is very well illustrated, and the concepts are easy to take home. Home and library use of this book will improve the child, parent, and school system."

— **Shirley Gutkowski, RDH,** Practice Limited to Orofacial Myofunctional Therapy

"What a cute way to deliver such important information to our young ones. Dr. Diehnelt is a compassionate dentist who makes her point clearly in a fun way."

— **Dr. Sandra Kahn** - CEO of Forwardontics

"This charming, illustrated children's book tells the important story of airway problems and how they can be the source of crowded teeth. For most of the story Alex believes his "jeans" (mistaken for genes) are the cause. Thank you Dr. Diehnelt for being a missionary for healthier children and presenting this important message in a simple and easy to understand way. In 2024, most people still believe crooked teeth are genetic, there is nothing to do about it -- just wait until the age of 12 and correct with braces and maybe extractions to fit big teeth in a small mouth. *My Jeans* alerts to the fact there are multiple causes which present from birth that could and should be identified and treated before the age of 6. I believe many readers will seek more information and uncover their child's hidden airway / breathing issue and pursue early and comprehensive treatment."

— **Howard G. Hindin, DDS,**
President, American Academy of Physiological Medicine & Dentistry
Director, Foundation for Airway Health
Author, *GASP: Airway Health - The Hidden Path to Wellness*

"This charming book addresses a timely and important issue affecting a huge population of people worldwide. Written in layman's terms, and with a touch of humor, this engaging yet educational book focuses on a crucial component of good health and appearance. The illustrations are current, fitting the narrative perfectly."

"*My Jeans?* would be a terrific addition to any home, library and/ or health care provider's office. Great gift!"
— "Well done Dr. Diehnelt!!"

— **Cindy Archilles, RDH, OMT**

Dedicated to those who seek the truth

"Mom, why are my teeth crooked?"

"It's your genes," she answered.

My jeans? I haven't worn them lately.

It's been too hot. I'll have to look for them.

I found them. I love my old jeans.

Oh, they are a bit tight and too short for me now.
Why would these jeans make my
teeth crooked? I don't get it.

I know. I'll visit Tommy next door. He has
straight teeth. What are his jeans like?

"Knock, knock. Anybody home?"

"Hi, Alex!"

"Do you have jeans?" I asked.

"No, they're not my style," she said with a smile.

"Is Tommy home?"

"Yeah. He's in his room. Come on in."
"Tommy! Alex is here for you."

"Can I see your jeans?" I asked.

"No problem."

"Here they are!"

"My Mom said I have crooked teeth 'cuz of my jeans.
You have nice straight teeth. Can I try on your jeans?"

"Sure, go ahead"

"These are a bit big for me, but..."

"They are too small for me now. If you want, you can have them," Tommy told me.

"Really? This is great. Jeans I can
smile with. Thanks, Tommy."

"Alex, where did you get those jeans? Isn't it a hot day for jeans?" Mom questioned me.

"Oh, Tommy gave them to me. Now, I can smile big like him. You told me I had bad jeans, so I got new ones."

Mom replied, "Actually, I think you got your bad genes from your grandpa. He has big teeth."

I thought my mom bought my jeans last year...

I know. I'll check the photos of Grandpa growing up. That's a smart idea.

Grandpa was a cute boy, but I just don't see him ever wearing jeans. I don't see anyone wearing jeans back then. They sure had funny clothes!

I am really confused now...

"Mom, can we visit Grandpa tomorrow?"

"I'd love to. We can leave right after
lunch," she responded.

"Grandpa, do you wear jeans?"

"No, Alex, I prefer these pants. Why do you ask?"

"Mom told me I had crooked teeth because of my jeans, and then she said I got my bad jeans from YOU. This is crazy. I don't want crooked teeth!"

Grandpa chuckled lightly, and then said, "I can see why it doesn't make any sense, poor boy. Let me explain."

I let out a sigh of relief.

"Jeans don't cause crooked teeth. Your jeans, my jeans or anyone else's jeans.

"What? You mean Mom lied to me? Why?" I questioned as my face became red with anger.

Grandpa replied in a calming manner, "You have every right to be upset. Your mom didn't know. She told you what most people believe."

"That means that everybody is wrong." I deduced.

"Bingo! You got it. **Almost** everybody is wrong."

"So what is the truth?"

"First, I need to explain that there are two totally different kinds of jeans. I'm not talking about different styles or colors of jeans. There are the jeans you wear. These are J E A N S.

"Ah, huh" I muttered.

Grandpa continued, "Then there are "genes" which are parts of your body that determine how tall you grow and what kind of hair you have. These are spelled G E N E S. It sounds just like the jeans you wear, but it means something totally different. I can see why you were confused."

"I'm not a good speller."

"That's OK. You don't need to be. When your mom said that you had crooked teeth because of your genes, she meant that your body was created to be that way, and nothing would change that."

"So, she was talking about my body, and I thought she was talking about clothes."

"Exactly. It's starting to make sense now, Alex, isn't it?"

"Yup".

"Most people today, like your Mom, think that teeth are crooked because of the genes in the family. For example, you got big teeth like your grandfather and small jaws from your mother. But this is NOT true. Most people have not learned the truth.

"Then, Grandpa, honestly, truly, why do I have crooked teeth?" I pleaded.

"Are you ready for a surprise?"

"It can't be worse than what I've been through already."

"You get crooked teeth because of how you breathe, how you swallow, and what you eat. This is the real truth."

"For real? I never heard that. Are you sure?"

"While I've been explaining this to you, you've had your lips apart and been breathing through your mouth. You should breathe through your nose. That's why you have crooked teeth."

"Is it that simple?" I asked in disbelief.

"Sure is. From here on out, make sure you breathe through your nose. You won't catch colds as often, and you'll be healthier."

"Will I have straight teeth then?"

"It will be a great start, but there will
be a lot more work to do."

"I got these jeans from Tommy because I thought
they would give me straight teeth. It doesn't make
sense for me to keep wearing them now, does it?"

"Wear whatever you want. Next time you see Tommy, check and see if he has his mouth closed. We know he's been breathing through his nose."

"This makes sense. I wish I had known this earlier. Thank you."

"You're welcome. It's always great to see you, and I'm so glad I was able to help. Now you can help spread the truth, too.

"Love you!"

RESOURCES

Websites:

www.airwayhealth.org Foundation for Airway Health

www.aapmd.org The American Academy of Physiological Medicine & Dentistry

www.aago.com Academy of Airway and Gnathological Orthopedics

www.aomtinfo.org Academy of Orofacial Myofunctional Therapy

www.myoresearch.com Myofunctional Research Co.

www.westonaprice.org The Weston A. Price Foundation

www.serenityhealthysmiles.com Serenity Healthy Smiles

Books:

Jaws by Sandra Kahn and Paul R. Ehrlich
Breath by James Nestor
Gasp by Michael Gelb and Howard Hindin
The Oxygen Advantage by Patrick McKeown
The Dental Diet by Steven Lin
Nutrition and Physical Degeneration by Weston A. Price
Shut Your Mouth and Save Your Life by George Catlin

Grandpa

Printed in the United States
by Baker & Taylor Publisher Services